Saving the Zog

Helen Strahinich

Illustrated by Scott Angle

www.steck-vaughn.com

ISBN 0-7398-5104-7

Printed in the United States of America.

1 2 3 4 5 6 7 8 9 LB 06 05 04 03 02

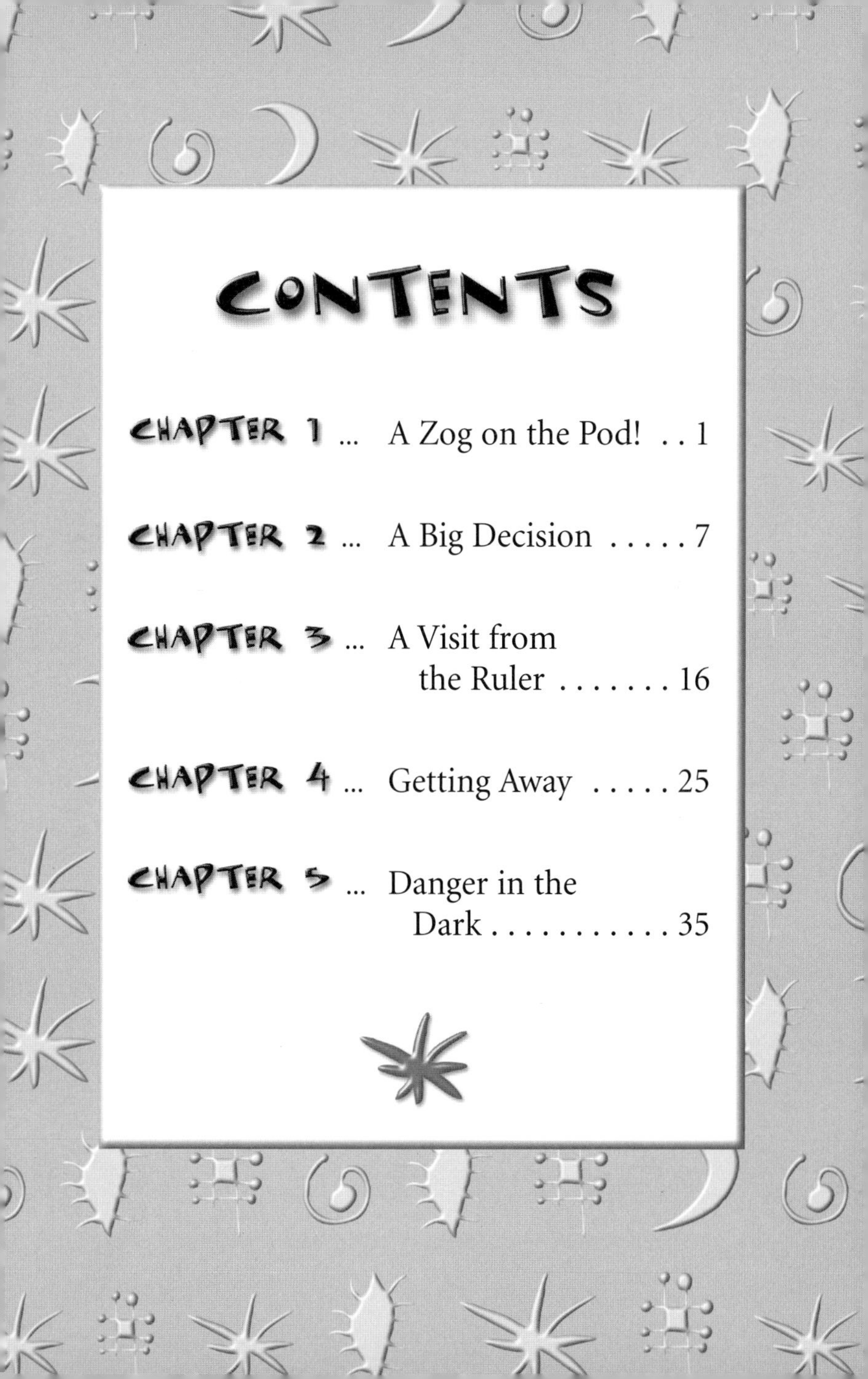

CONTENTS

CHAPTER 1

A ZOG ON THE POD!

This morning began like every other morning. When I woke up, I joined my family in the common room. Together, we recited the Pod Rules:

"Always remember the good of the Pod.

The Pod feeds the Pod, and the Pod helps the Pod.

Secrets hurt the Pod, and strangers hurt the Pod.

The Pod is all for one, and the Pod is one for all."

Then, I hurried into the garden to pick bread berries for breakfast.

The purple sky of planet Tolup was clear. The twin orange suns blazed like monsters' eyes.

When I heard a familiar flapping sound, I turned and smiled. It was my pet Potok, Gova. He flew across the garden and landed on my shoulder. I ran my hand over Gova's soft, orange feathers. His long, purple beak hooked over his blue grin.

Good morning, Sasha, Gova thought.

Good morning, Gova, I thought back.

Gova and I don't communicate by talking. When we want to share our thoughts, I can "hear" his, and he can "hear" mine.

I'm flying off now, Gova told me.

Have a nice trip around the Pod, I answered.

After Gova flew away, I turned back to the bread berry bush. I was careful not to drop any berries, because food on our Pod is so scarce. We need every last berry we can find.

Just then, I heard a sound like a hiccup. It came from the round tent where my parents keep our garden tools and seeds. I figured some animal must be raiding our seeds, so I raced toward the tent, shouting.

But when I stepped through the tent's flap, I saw a very strange boy curled up in the corner. He had red eyes, green skin, and a pointy chin. His long ears poked through his curly green hair.

My own hair is blue, and my eyes are yellow, the same as the others on my Pod. That's how I knew right away that he was a Zog. I had never seen one before.

My first reaction was to jump back. But the boy called out, "Help me!"

His words stopped me cold. The boy sounded the same as everyone on my Pod!

"You're a Zog, aren't you?" I asked. The boy nodded.

I'd heard about the Zogs. They owned tiny farms outside the Pods of Eastland, where I lived. The Rulers of Eastland hated the Zogs. The Rulers had forced the Zogs to give up most of their crops. Many Zogs were now starving.

"I'm so hungry!" the Zog cried out.

I knew I shouldn't feed the boy without permission, but he looked so thin. I took out a handful of bread berries and set them on a flat stone that my father uses to grind seeds.

"My name is Sasha," I said.

"I'm Jared," he answered. He finished the berries in a breath.

"Where are your parents?" I asked him.

"I don't know!" he replied. "Last night, we were trying to cross your Pod. We thought a Pod girl had seen us, and we got scared. When we ran to hide, I got lost. My parents told me to find the Pod of Goodell if we ever got separated. Will you help me contact Goodell?"

The Rules of the Pod demanded that I say no. I had heard of a Pod that had helped some Zogs once. When the Rulers found out, they broke up the Pod and took over the land. Without land to grow food on, many of those Pod folk died.

My parents had taught me to respect the Rules of the Pod. But they also had taught me to treat others as I would like to be treated. Did they mean Zogs, too?

"Wait for me here, Jared," I said. "I'll be back as soon as I can."

I knew I'd be back. What I hadn't decided was whether I'd bring the authorities.

A Big Decision

After breakfast, I had no chance to think about what to do. “Get going or you’ll be late for school,” my mother said.

I headed down the front path with my sister, Talia, as I did every day. But this was no ordinary day. My mind was on Jared, hiding in our tent.

“What’s wrong with you, Sasha?” Talia asked, poking me in the arm. “You’ve been pouting since you woke up. Are you still mad that I lost your orange nose beads?”

Talia looked at me with her thin yellow eyes full of mischief. She loves to make trouble.

Should I tell Talia about our unexpected guest? What would she do? Luckily, my sister could not read my thoughts, as Gova could.

Before I had a chance to speak, Talia shouted, "The Ping Tree has blossomed! It's the first one on the Pod!"

We both raced toward the good-luck Ping Tree at the bottom of the path. It was near the entrance to the underground winter passage.

The new red Ping cones would bring great happiness to everyone in our home.

We stopped to fill our book bags with the Ping cones. Now we were really late for school. "Last one there's a rotten Potok egg!" my sister shouted, and off she ran.

We raced past the other small round houses on the path that circled Town Center. We reached the School House in record time. We ran in just as the Top Teacher rang the morning bell.

The first class was Gymnasia, my favorite. Today we were playing my very best sport, Deloop. But I couldn't concentrate on our game at all. I was thinking about poor Jared. Would he try to cross the Pod by himself? What if someone caught him? The least I could do was bring him some food.

Twice I dropped the ball. Then I slammed right into my teammate.

"Watch where you're going!" he shouted.

That gave me an idea. The next time a player passed me, I ran into her. Then I dropped to the ground.

When my Pod mates surrounded me, I howled, "Something's wrong with my shoulder."

Soon afterwards, I was on my way home in the nurse's pedal cart.

"Let me help you to the door," the nurse said.

"I can make it myself!" I told her quickly, hoping my mother had not seen us.

As soon as the nurse drove off in the pedal cart, I rushed to the garden tent. My heart raced as I pushed through the tent flap. What if someone had discovered the Zog?

I didn't see Jared at first, so I whispered his name. When he didn't answer, my throat tightened. I was afraid the worst had happened.

Jared was just hiding behind a barrel. He crept up to my side, and I smiled with relief.

We sat down on the flat grinding stone. I took my lunch from my book bag and shared it with Jared. I knew I'd get nothing else to eat before dinner. I also knew I was breaking Pod Rules.

Then I dug into my book bag again. “This Ping cone is for you,” I said, placing a cone in Jared’s hand. “I hope it brings you good luck. It sounds like you need it.”

“It’s been terrible for all the Zogs,” he said, his lips shaking. “The Rulers of Eastland hate us.”

"But the Pod of Goodell helps Zogs?" I asked.

"They've helped many Zogs escape to Westland," Jared said. "Their Pod is near the edge of Westland, and they help us sneak past the Eastland guards."

"So you and your family were trying to get to Westland," I guessed.

"Yes, the Rulers of Westland welcome the Zogs," he answered. "Not everybody in Westland lives on a Pod, as most people do here in Eastland. Many people in Westland live like we Zogs do."

"Then I have to contact the Pod of Goodell so they can bring you to Westland," I said. I tried to sound sure of myself, but I had no plan at all.

"Does that mean you're going to help me?" Jared asked, trying not to look too hopeful. I nodded. He gave me a warm Zog smile.

I knew I had to try to get Jared to safety. He was separated from his people, and there was no one else to help him. If I were lost, I'd want someone to help me.

Then I thought of a plan! "There's an underground passage," I said. "Nobody is using it now because the weather's warm. It's only used during the cold season, when the Pod is covered with ice and it's dangerous to walk outdoors. You can hide there until I can get a message to the Pod of Goodell."

Just then, I heard the door of our house slam shut. I jumped up and looked out the tent flap. To my horror, I saw my mother step outside.

She didn't stop to dig in our garden. She didn't stop to pick bread berries or milk roots. She didn't stop by the water pool. My mother was heading up the pathway toward the tool tent, straight toward us!

A VISIT FROM THE RULER

My mother stood just a few feet away. I expected her to burst through the tent flap any second. The only place to hide was behind the big barrel, but there was only room for one. I pushed Jared behind it.

What would I tell my mother? How could I explain my absence from school? I only hoped she'd be so angry when she saw me here that she wouldn't discover the Zog.

Luckily, my mother stopped outside the tent. "I wish those kids would learn to clean up after themselves," she grumbled.

"I ask them to put away the garden equipment until I'm purple in the face," she said. "They never think about the rest of us!"

I heard her pick up a shovel and start to dig for milk roots. Jared let out a hiccup and the digging stopped. I clapped my hand over his mouth.

But then the digging started again.

When the digging sounds got farther away, I said, "That was close! I have to get you to the passage tonight. If you're caught here, the Rulers will punish my whole Pod."

I peeked out of the tent flap and saw my mother digging far off in the north field. I slipped back to the house and went to my room. Gova flew toward me and landed on my shoulder. Usually, I didn't even notice his weight, but today it felt like a heavy burden.

You have troubles on your mind, Gova thought.

I nodded.

Do you wish to share them? he asked.

Not now, Gova, I said, thinking he might disapprove.

You see, Gova is a completely good creature, so it was possible that he would want me to help Jared. But Gova's job is to keep me out of trouble, so it was also possible that he wouldn't help at all.

Most days, Gova would have pushed me to explain. Today he didn't. I was afraid that my worries would let my secret thoughts leak out. If Gova heard them, what would he do?

Talia returned from the School House a short time later. Like Gova, my sister had questions. "So how are you feeling now?" she asked slyly.

"My shoulder is much better," I said.

Talia gave me a funny look and said, "I think you just wanted a day off from school. What will you give me if I don't tell?"

I shook my head, but I didn't dare say a word. I was afraid my voice would give me away.

"Admit it," Talia said, "you skipped school today." She leaned close to my face. "Why?"

Talia herself had skipped school the week before. She got caught and she was punished.

“You’re the one who skips,” I snapped, “not me.”

Talia was about to answer, but my mother interrupted us, much to my relief. “Time for the Pod meeting,” she called.

Talia made a face at me and poked out her bright blue tongue. “Maybe I’ll tell, maybe I won’t,” she said. “I’ll find out what you were doing. Then I’ll decide.”

“Let’s get going!” my mother called.

I raced out of the room, ending my talk with Talia.

Father joined us at the door, and we all walked together to the big, round Meeting House.

All two hundred members of our Pod were in the hall when we arrived. We sat down under the giant canopy that covered the round space.

Under the edge of the canopy, I could see thick pink clouds that meant we'd soon have water spill. Most evenings, I would have welcomed water spill for our crops. But I wished for clear purple skies tonight, so that the Zog and I could travel to the underground passage without difficulty.

Someone shook the bells, and we stood to recite the Pod Rules. "Always remember the good of the Pod. The Pod feeds the Pod...." I mouthed the words, but I felt like a fake. I was feeding a Zog who was hiding in my own garden!

We all sat down to hear the reading of the week's Plan Book. Then, a sudden thunder of drums filled the air. Those drums meant that a Ruler of Eastland was about to enter. We all jumped to our feet again.

The Ruler marched from the back of the hall down an aisle in the center. We watched him walk to the front in his long, gray robe. Why was a Ruler visiting our Pod today? Usually, such a visit was planned at least a moon before it happened. My heart pounded.

The Ruler raised his arms to tell us to be seated and to quiet the whispering. Suddenly, the room was as silent as Gova's voice.

“Good afternoon, Pod citizens,” he said kindly. “I wish you all a rich growing season and full bellies.” Laughter rang through the Meeting House, and he smiled.

“But I haven’t come to trade small talk with you,” he said. His smile disappeared. “We believe that there are Zogs on your Pod.”

Everyone in the hall gasped at once and then began whispering. Our Ruler held up his arms for silence. “I’ve come to ask whether you’ve seen anything unusual.”

A hush fell over us, and we all looked around from neighbor to neighbor, Pod mate to Pod mate. I felt my vital liquid rush to my face. A chill rose along the hairs of my neck. For a long moment, no one said a word. I took a deep breath of relief.

Before I could take another breath, I saw a hand rise right beside me. It belonged to a girl named Babba. She sat at my lunch table and was in my Gymnasia class. Now Babba was waving her hand like a blue flag!

Getting Away

"Yes, Pod Sister, what can you tell us?" the Ruler asked Babba.

Babba stood to address our Ruler. "Great Ruler, this morning I thought I saw two strange green animals near the Supply House. I believed my eyes were playing tricks on me, but now I'm not sure."

"Thank you, Pod Sister, for your sharp observation," he said.

Our Ruler clapped his hands three times. Two guards stood and approached him. He spoke to them quietly, and the guards hurried out.

Our Ruler faced us again. Now his eyes burned with an angry fire. "I warn you that your Pod is in danger until the Zogs are found. We will not stand by and let your Pod help Zogs! If you want to keep your lands and feed your children, watch carefully and report anything strange that you might see."

Why should they hate the Zogs so much? It wasn't fair! Jared was alone and helpless. I had to help him, and that was that. But I feared deeply for myself, for my family, and for my Pod.

When my family returned home, we had dinner together at a table outside our back door. I was terribly hungry, but I couldn't make myself eat. My stomach was in knots. I slipped my milk roots and sweet grains into my pocket. Jared would need them.

"I don't feel well," I told my parents.

My sister threw me a curious look. “Why is Sasha sneaking food?” she asked loudly.

Everyone looked at me. “I was going to eat it,” I said quickly. With all eyes on me, I had no choice. I ate the milk roots. I couldn’t let anyone get too curious.

Then I went to my sleep room to think. Outside my window, clouds covered the stars and both moons. That was good. Jared and I could travel more safely without the bright moonlight. But I hoped that there would be no water spill tonight.

My plan was now more dangerous than ever. Our Ruler had made it clear that helping a Zog would endanger the Pod. I took out some paper and wrote a short note to the leader of the Pod of Goodell.

Then my thoughts called Gova to carry the letter for me. But would Gova help? I had to take the chance. I could never make the trip myself.

Gova landed on my shoulder. I explained how I planned to help the Zog and why.

Gova looked at me for a moment. *I'm proud of you, Sasha,* he said. *You've chosen a noble path.*

I ran my hand gently over Gova's feathers. Then I gave him my sealed letter. He took it in his long beak. I opened the window, and Gova flew into the dark night toward the Pod of Goodell.

May good luck travel with you, Gova, I thought after him.

May your goodness keep your heart strong, he thought back. I watched until I couldn't see or hear Gova any longer.

I put out my light stick, lay down on my sleep board, and pretended to sleep. Then I heard a knock on my door.

"Sasha?" It was Talia. "I'm sorry I told on you at dinner," she said. "What are you up to? Please tell me."

I was dying to tell somebody. I didn't want to carry this burden all alone. But I didn't want to involve my sister in it, even if she was a pain sometimes.

"I promise I'll tell you tomorrow, Talia. Just not tonight," I said.

"You'd better," she answered, and then she went away.

Finally, all the light sticks in the house were out. I could hear my father and mother snoring in the next room. I got up and folded a blanket over my arm. Then I slipped out of the house.

I hurried inside the garden tent. "Jared," I whispered, "are you ready to go?"

He came out from behind the barrel.

"We have to hurry," I said. "A Ruler is on our Pod with a patrol. There are guards everywhere! Follow me and don't you dare let out a hiccup!"

Jared held my hand tightly while I led him toward the Town Center. Just as we neared the Supply House, I saw a group of guards. I knew of an entrance at the far side of our School House, on the opposite end of Town Center. But first we had to get there.

A bolt of lightning streaked across the sky, brightening everything in sight, including ourselves.

We hurried onto a dark side path. Few people ever used this path, even during the day. The ground was covered with tall weeds, so we were hidden from view.

The path took us safely around the Town Center to the back of my school.

We entered the School Grounds and raced across them. Large drops of water splattered us. Then the skies opened up. The water spill fell heavily.

In the distance, I heard guards calling, but I couldn't make out their words. Were they shouting at us? I hoped they couldn't see us through the water spill.

Finally, we reached the entrance to the passage. No guards were in sight. We slipped through the round door.

The passage was dark, so I turned on my light stick. I'd never seen it dark like this. In the winter, many light sticks brighten the passage. Then it was easy to see far ahead. Now it was so dark that I could only see one foot in front of me.

Yet I knew this passage as well as I knew my own garden. I led Jared to a little spot off the main tunnel. Talia and I sometimes sat there in the winter to talk by ourselves.

I laid down the blanket for Jared in a dry corner. We were both dripping wet.

"Have hope," I said. "My Potok is flying a letter to the Pod of Goodell tonight. I'll be back for you tomorrow. Don't worry."

That's what I told Jared, but I was full of worries. Jared was counting on me. I hadn't even been able to bring him food. What if I couldn't keep him safe? What if the Pod of Goodell didn't really help Zogs? What if I couldn't get him there?

DANGER IN THE DARK

My next day at school seemed to last for a thousand moons. I couldn't stop worrying about Jared, alone and hungry in that dark passage.

To make matters worse, Gova had not returned from his trip to the Pod of Goodell with my letter. He had never before stayed away from home all night. I had no idea whether he was alive or dead. Had the trip been too far for him? Had the patrol captured him and read the letter?

When I walked through the door of our house after school, my mother greeted me with a worried hug. "Gova doesn't seem well," she said.

"Where is he?" I asked. My heart beat faster than Gova's wings in flight.

"In your sleep room," my mother said.

I raced in to check on Gova, who was fast asleep on my sleep board. I sat beside him and patted his head. Gova opened one eye.

Are you sick? I asked.

I'm exhausted, he replied. *I left a letter from the Pod of Goodell under your pillow.*

I felt under my pillow and pulled out the letter. Inside were directions for how to reach a meeting place after dark.

The hours before that night's sleep time passed as slowly as our winter. But at last, dinner was eaten, homework was finished, and every light stick in our home was turned off. My family was fast asleep on their sleep boards.

Only Gova and I were awake, sitting at the window and looking for guards in the light of our two orange moons.

I believe we can travel safely now, Gova said.

That's just what I was thinking, I answered.

Gova and I studied the map that the Pod of Goodell had made for us. I stole some food from the kitchen. Then we slipped out of the house.

Gova flew ahead of me toward the tunnel. Along the way, I stopped twice when I thought I heard the sound of footsteps. Each time, I decided that my ears were playing tricks on me.

We reached our destination with a small bag of food for Jared. He lay in the corner where I'd left him, looking pale.

I whispered, "Jared, we're here to take you to the Pod of Goodell."

"I think I'm sick," he moaned.

"I've brought you food," I told him. "You'll feel better after you've eaten."

Just then, I thought I heard footsteps in the main passage. I put my finger over my lips to warn Jared not to speak. We listened, but we heard nothing. Was I hearing things again?

Jared ate in silence, chewing the milk roots quietly. The food must have been what he needed, for the green coloring returned to his face. Soon, he was ready to begin the trip.

Gova flew ahead of us in the dark tunnel to make sure the way was clear. We hurried along behind him. Again, I heard footsteps, and this time I was certain that someone else was in the passage.

What could I do now? Stop and hide? If guards were tracking us, there would be no hiding, no escape. Perhaps we should send Jared ahead on his own and then try to keep the guards from finding him.

But the guards would never believe that I had come to the tunnel for any other purpose than to help Zogs. The Rulers would take our land. All my Pod mates, young and old, would starve. It would all be my fault!

As we ran faster toward the exit, the footsteps sounded closer. "We're almost there," I said, "but we have to hurry." As we rushed out of the tunnel, I heard a voice behind us calling my name. It sounded familiar, but how could that be?

I heard the voice again and realized that it belonged to my father!

I stopped and turned around. “How long have you been following us? And…why?” I asked, my voice cracking with fear.

I knew my father would be angry that I had helped a Zog. But what would he do to Jared? I considered telling Jared to run for his life, but he couldn’t run faster than my father.

My father stepped close to me, and I saw his face in the glow of my light stick. To my great surprise, he was smiling. His eyes sparkled with pride.

“My dear daughter,” he said. “I’ve been wondering what you were up to these past few days. Then I heard about your letter to the Pod of Goodell.”

“How did you hear?” I asked, amazed.

"Your mother and I have many friends there. We've been working to save the Zogs for a long time. Our friends at Goodell wanted to be sure that you were safe. They were very impressed that a young girl would face such danger by herself."

"I'm sorry, Father. I know I should have told you."

"You should have warned your mother and me, but I guess we were keeping secrets of our own," my father said. "I understand why you were afraid to speak of the Zog." Then he glanced over at Jared. "Won't you introduce me to your friend?"

Friend? Yes, I liked that word! Friend!

"Father, this is Jared," I said. Jared held up his hand for my father to shake.

"I heard from the Pod of Goodell that your parents arrived there two days ago, safe and sound," my father said. "They'll be overjoyed to hear that you're alive and well."

Jared smiled.

We reached the meeting place before dawn. Several people from the Pod of Goodell met us. In the half-light, we all shook hands.

"You've raised your daughter well," the leader of Goodell told my father. Then, he turned to me. "You're a very brave girl," he told me. "May your good deeds bring you happiness in the future."

"Our movement is growing," my father said.

"It is indeed," said the leader of Goodell. "More and more Pod folks want to help the Zogs every day. Each time we save a Zog from the evil Rulers of Eastland, we feel more sure that we are on the right track."

In the first rays of dawn, my father, Gova, and I said farewell to Jared. He flashed me a warm Zog smile.

"Thanks, Sasha!" he said. "I wish we didn't have to say good-bye."

But Jared was safe. I knew that helping the Zog had been the right thing to do.